Smythe Gambrell Library

Presented by

Sage Gupta

in honor of my sister,

Sky Gupta

Spring 2015

Three Names of Me

Mary Cummings

Illustrated by **Lin Wang**

Albert Whitman & Company
Morton Grove, Illinois

Library of Congress Cataloging-in-Publication Data

Cummings, Mary.
Three names of me / written by Mary Cummings ; illustrated by Lin Wang.
p. cm.
Summary: A girl adopted from China explains that her three names—one her birth mother whispered
in her ear, one the babysitters at her orphanage called her, and one her American parents gave her—are
each an important part of who she is. Includes scrapbooking ideas for other girls adopted from China.
ISBN-10: 0-8075-7903-3 (hardcover)
ISBN-13: 978-0-8075-7903-9 (hardcover)
[1. Names, Personal—Fiction. 2. Adoption—Fiction. 3. Chinese Americans—Fiction.]
I. Wang, Lin, 1973- , ill. II. Title.
PZ7.C9147Thr 2006 [E]—dc22 2006004725

The design is by Carol Gildar.

For more information about Albert Whitman & Company,
please visit our web site at www.albertwhitman.com.

For Ada, and for all the names that are you. —M.C.

For Willson and Megan. —L.W.

Ada Lorane Bennett. That is my name.
But it is not the first name I've had.
It is the third.

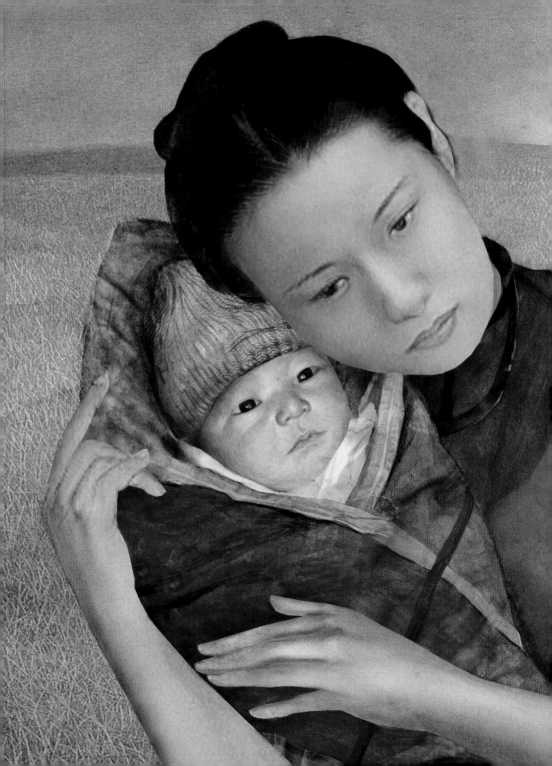

My first name was whispered to me
by my first mother, when I was born.
It's someplace in my heart.
I don't know how to say it. I wish I could.

I didn't see my first mother long.
  I never saw her again.
      I am from someone I don't even know.

She is my China mother,
and far away I have a father, too.
They made my hands and my eyes
and my dark hair,
all the parts of me I can touch and see.

But they took me to an orphanage.
I don't know just why.
My heart tells me they were sad.
China is crowded and not rich.
It has rules about how many
children a family can have.

At the orphanage,
I was given my second name:
Wang Bin.

Wang means I'm like a
Chinese princess.
Bin is for "gentle and refined."
The babysitters said that's
how I was.
But I don't remember
anything about them,
or that place,
or the tiny me.

"You will go to America," they said, and I didn't understand that, either.

The baby picture I like best
shows me in my orphanage sleep suit
in between the two people
who came to China
to be my mom and dad.

My mom lifted me up
so I could see us in a mirror.
Light glowed around us like sunshine.

We three flew high in an airplane,
in and out of gray clouds,
through the long night to America.
I napped and laughed with them,
and they gave me my third name: "Ada."
In Chinese that means "love arrived": *ai da*.

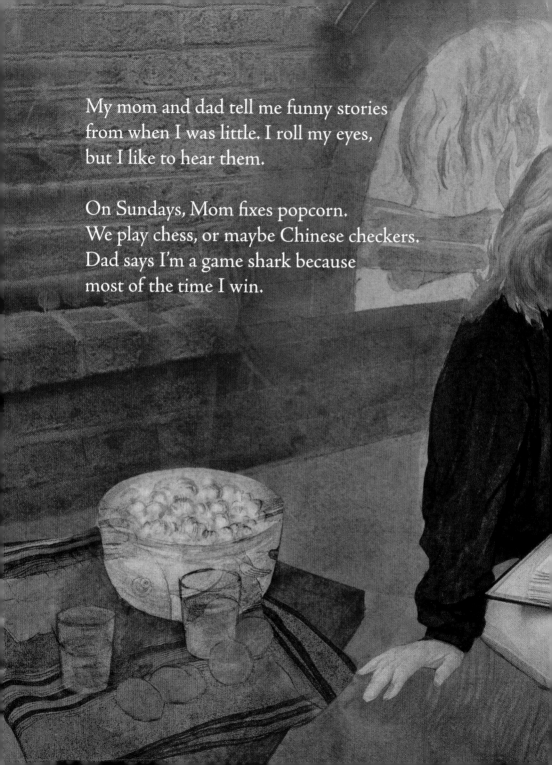

My mom and dad tell me funny stories
from when I was little. I roll my eyes,
but I like to hear them.

On Sundays, Mom fixes popcorn.
We play chess, or maybe Chinese checkers.
Dad says I'm a game shark because
most of the time I win.

At school, I put "Ada Bennett"
across the top of my papers.
But for special projects,
I take colored paper and markers
and use all the names of me I know:
        Ada
        Lorane
        Wang Bin
        Bennett

Ada is about love, so it gets a heart.
Lorane is for my two grandmothers,
Lorraine and Lorayne,
and I draw two smiles.

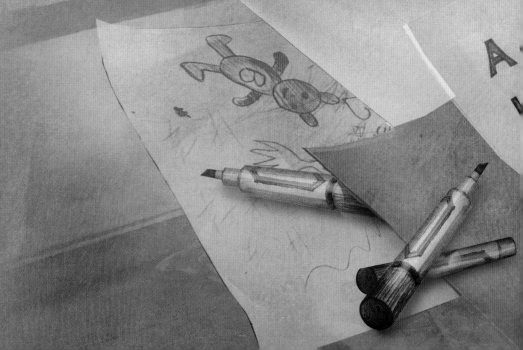

Wang and *Bin* get a crown,
for the refined Chinese princess part of me.
Bennett is our family name,
so it means Mom and Dad
and me.

But there is another name of me
that I don't know.
So I take glue and glitter
and my red marker.
I make a beautiful star
for the name I only heard once,
the name before my remembering.

Sometimes, after I'm tucked in bed at night,
I look out at the real stars.
They are very far away.
But they are still bright.
They shine on me and my mom and dad.
They shine on my China parents, too,
only not at the same time.
Do they think of me
when they look up at the night sky?

When they think I'm not looking,
some people stare at my mom and dad and me.
They stare because our skin and hair
and eyes don't match, and they wonder why that is.
I do not like to be stared at.
What I like are hot dogs, stuffed animals,
and roller coaster rides.

What I like are foggy mountains,
tiny pink flowers,
water buffaloes, and rice.
Is it because all of these come from my first home?

What I like is my red silk outfit
with the mandarin collar that I wear on holidays.
Red is the color of happiness
in the land where I was born,
and I carried happiness with me to this land.

What I am is a Chinese girl,
and my first country has the Great Wall
that is famous all around the world.

What I am is an American girl
who speaks English
and knows a few words of Chinese—

Thank you, Xie xie   Good-bye, Zai-jian   Hello, Ni hao

Love arrived, Ai da. Ada.

My first name is a bright red star
wrapped in my heart.
I heard it long ago, with love,
so it is still there.
Xie xie, first mother. Thank you.

My second name is from the land I was born in
and said good-bye to.
Zai-jian, China.
Good-bye from Wang Bin,
gentle and refined princess girl.

My third name is my *ni hao*, my hello,
full of love.
 I am love arrived in this place,
 this family. I am
  Ai da.
   Ada.

Hi!

Do you like to write in a journal?

Have you ever made a scrapbook about you?

Journals usually just have writing in them. Scrapbooks are art projects. Pictures with fancy edges or collage can be mixed with writing.

But it's up to you. Make your scrapbook any way you want!

Since you've been reading *Three Names of Me,* I'm sharing part of my own scrapbook because we probably have some things in common.

Mostly I write just whatever comes into my head or from my heart. Sometimes I ask other people (like my parents) when I don't know something that they probably do. The Internet has cool things about China, so I look there, too.

I like to make lists. I have lots of them in my scrapbook. OK. Here goes:

My Favorites

Color

Yellow

Friends

Leah and Brooke

Books

Fantasy stories with elves and wizards or about kung-fu warrior princesses.

Sports

Baseball (to watch) Soccer (to play)

Animals/pets

Henrietta, my aunt and uncle's terrier.

Mandy, the black-and-white mouse I used to have who died.

My Family

Foods

Peppermint bon-bon ice cream

Bow tie pasta with parmesan cheese

Only three people, plus a goldfish. No brothers or sisters.

We like music. I play guitar with my dad.

Dad's tall. Mom's medium-sized. I think I'll be medium-sized when I finish growing.

Ada is a Chinese name and an American name. The name is short, but in Chinese it has two characters. (Chinese doesn't use alphabet letters like we do. They have characters that combine pictures with word meanings.)

ADA

Ada

ADA

Ada

Ada

Love

The center part looks like a little smiley face, but it's supposed to be a heart.

Arrived

It looks like an "i" next to a tower. The "i" reminds me of a balloon on a string.

My list of WHATs

What I think would have been different about my life if I'd grown up in China

School would have been harder. I'd have to memorize all those characters with just the right kind of strokes and pieces.

My town would be more crowded than where I live now because there are lots of people in China.

Most people would look like me.

What I'd like to see or find out if I go to China someday

To learn how to paint Chinese-style pictures.

To see the Temple of Heaven in Beijing, where the emperors thanked heaven for being able to rule.

To see the orphanage where I was as a baby.

To find the people who took care of me.

What I like that's Chinese

ME!
Silk
Rice
Brush-paintings

Martial arts movies.
I want to learn to kick
  and leap like that someday.
    Pandas
        Chinese acrobats

What I'd like to be when I grow up

A marine biologist and
work with dolphins.

Year of the Dog

Y ou can make up your own lists
and questions in your scrapbook.
These are just mine.

   You can also search web sites by the name of the
province where you were born to learn more about China.
My birth province is Zhejiang. More than half of it is forest!
I learned about some famous places there, like the really old
Baoguo Temple where you can see traditional Chinese wedding
clothes. People in Zhejiang mostly eat fish, rice, vegetables, and
ham. Maybe some of my China relatives grow tea or rice or
maybe they are fishermen.

   If you search the computer under "Chinese Zodiac," you can
find the animal sign for the year you were born. There are twelve
animal signs. Mine is the Year of the Dog (but I don't have a dog!).
Your birth sign is repeated the year you turn twelve.

   Try "scrapbooking for kids" in your search engine on the
Internet to find ideas for your scrapbook.

                    Have fun!
                       Ada